Put Beginning Readers on the Right Track with
ALL ABOARD READING™

The All Aboard Reading series is especially designed for beginning readers. Written by noted authors and illustrated in full color, these are books that children really want to read—books to excite their imagination, expand their interests, make them laugh, and support their feelings. With fiction and nonfiction stories that are high interest and curriculum-related, All Aboard Reading books offer something for every young reader. And with four different reading levels, the All Aboard Reading series lets you choose which books are most appropriate for your children and their growing abilities.

Picture Readers
Picture Readers have super-simple texts, with many nouns appearing as rebus pictures. At the end of each book are 24 flash cards—on one side is a rebus picture; on the other side is the written-out word.

Station Stop 1
Station Stop 1 books are best for children who have just begun to read. Simple words and big type make these early reading experiences more comfortable. Picture clues help children to figure out the words on the page. Lots of repetition throughout the text helps children to predict the next word or phrase—an essential step in developing word recognition.

Station Stop 2
Station Stop 2 books are written specifically for children who are reading with help. Short sentences make it easier for early readers to understand what they are reading. Simple plots and simple dialogue help children with reading comprehension.

Station Stop 3
Station Stop 3 books are perfect for children who are reading alone. With longer text and harder words, these books appeal to children who have mastered basic reading skills. More complex stories captivate children who are ready for more challenging books.

In addition to All Aboard Reading books, look for All Aboard Math Readers™ (fiction stories that teach math concepts children are learning in school); All Aboard Science Readers™ (nonfiction books that explore the most fascinating science topics in age-appropriate language); and All Aboard Poetry Readers™ (funny, rhyming poems for readers of all levels).

All Aboard for happy reading!

To Randi and Robin—S.A.

To Shannon Flynn Bird—A.F.

Library of Congress Cataloging-in-Publication Data

Albert, Shirley.
    Doll party / by Shirley Albert ; illustrated by Amy Flynn.
       p.   cm.—(All aboard reading) "Level 1, Preschool—Grade 1."
    Summary: Becky, a young mouse, gets a new dolly and invites her friends for a doll party.
    [1. Dolls—Fiction.   2. Parties—Fiction.   3. Mice—Fiction.]
  I. Flynn, Amy, ill. II. Title. III. Series.
  PZ7.A3214Do 1994
  [E]—dc20   93-12685
                                                            CIP
                                                            AC

ISBN 0-448-40182-7

J

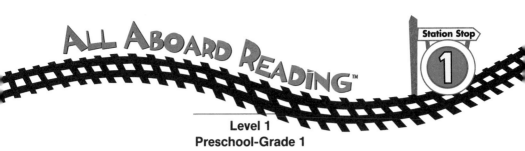
Doll Party

By Shirley Albert
Illustrated by Amy Flynn

Grosset & Dunlap • New York

"Look, Becky!" says Papa.
"It's a surprise
from Grandma."

It's a new doll.

The doll has a pretty dress
with roses on it.

And a big pink bow.

"May I have a party?"
Becky asks Mama.
"A party for my
pretty new dolly?"

"Yes," says Mama.
"You may have a party.
Go ask your friends.
But leave your dolly here.
You do not want her
to get dirty."

"I will be careful,"
says Becky.
Then she goes skipping
down the road
to see her friends.

First Becky goes
to Nan's house.
Nan is baking cookies.
"Will you come to a party
for my dolly tomorrow?"
asks Becky.

"Yes," says Nan. "I will.

Will you help me bake cookies?"

"Yes," says Becky.

So Becky and her dolly help.

Then Becky skips
to Mary's house.
"Oh, no," says Becky.
"My dolly is full of flour.
I must be more careful."

Mary is busy
in the garden.
"Will you come to a party
for my dolly tomorrow?"
Becky asks her friend.

"Yes," says Mary. "I will.

Will you help me

water these flowers?"

"Yes," says Becky.

So Becky and her dolly help.

Then Becky skips
to Jill's house.
"Oh, no," says Becky.
"My dolly has dirt on her dress.
I must be more careful."

Becky finds Jill
in the attic.
Becky asks her
to the party, too.

"Yes," says Jill. "I will come.

Will you help me dust?"

"Yes," says Becky.

So Becky and her dolly help.

Then Becky skips home.
"Oh, no," she says.
"My dolly is very dusty.
I must be more careful."

Hop, skip, hop.

Oops!

Becky trips.

She lands in the mud.

So does her dolly.

Now there is mud

and dust

and dirt

and flour

all over her new dolly.

Becky cries

all the way home.

"Do not cry,"
Mama tells her.
First she gives
Becky a bath.
And Becky gives
her dolly a bath.

Mama washes
the dolly's dress and bow.
Becky hangs them out to dry.

Later Becky dresses
her dolly again.
She looks almost
as good as new.

That night
Becky sleeps with her dolly.
She hugs her and says,
"I will name you Dora."

The next day
Becky gets dressed up
for the party.

Nan brings her doll
and a bag of cookies.
Mary brings her doll
and a bunch of flowers.
Jill brings her doll
and a little tea set
that she found
in the attic.
It is the best
doll party ever.

"I love you, Dora,"

says Becky.